Holes
and
Peeks

Ann Jonas

Greenwillow Books
New York

For Amy

Library of Congress Cataloging in
Publication Data

Jonas, Ann. Holes and peeks.

Summary: A young child is afraid of holes
unless they are fixed, plugged, or made
smaller, but he thinks "peeks" are fun
because he can see things through them.
[1. Size and shape—Fiction]
I. Title.
PZ7.J664Ho 1984   [E]   83-14128
ISBN 0-688-02537-4
ISBN 0-688-02538-2 (lib. bdg.)

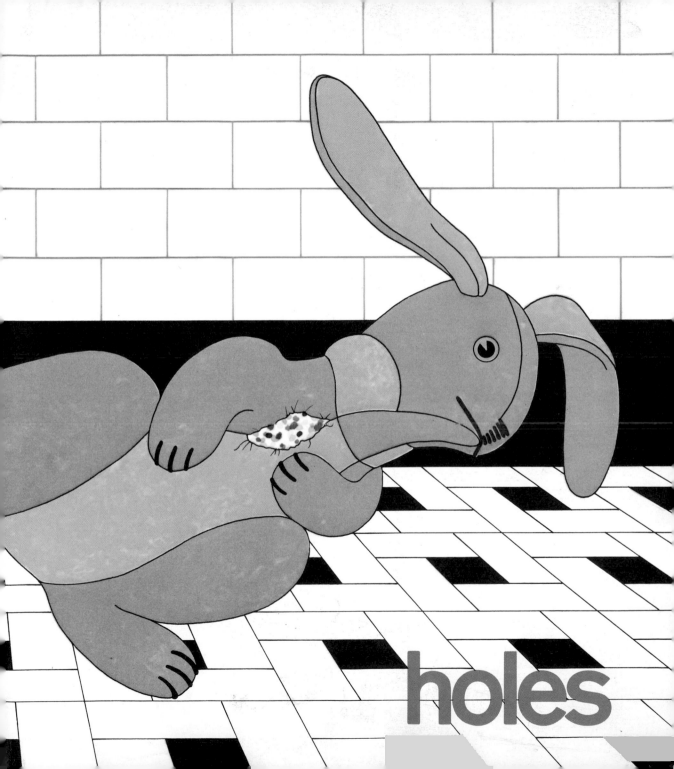

holes

holes. I don't like holes.

They scare me.

Peeks are different.
I can make peeks
and I can see things through them.

I can
watch my daddy
through a peek.

I can scare my mother

or my cat.

But if holes
are fixed,

or plugged,

they don't
scare me
anymore.

I might even
close the door
(but I'll leave a peek).